엘리트 시선 33

달빛으로 피는 박꽃

장현경 시집

엘리트출판사

이 도서의 국립중앙도서관 출판예정도서목록(CIP)은
서지정보유통지원시스템 홈페이지(http://seoji.nl.go.kr)와
국가자료종합목록 구축시스템(http://kolis-net.nl.go.kr)에서 이용하실 수 있습니다.
(CIP제어번호 : CIP2020013897)

달빛으로 피는 박꽃

장현경 시집

엘리트출판사

극기복례(克己復禮)가 인(仁)이다

공자(孔子)가 논어에서 말하기를 극기복례(克己復禮)가 인(仁)이라고 했다. 즉 자신을 이기고 예로 돌아가는 것이 인이다. 넓게 보면 개인에 대한 욕심을 버리고 공공의 이익을 위해 사회적 질서인 예를 회복시키는 것을 말한다.

공자왈(孔子曰)
지사인인(志士仁人) 무구생이해인(無求生以害仁) 유살신이성인(有殺身以成仁)
공자(孔子)가 이르기를
"지사(志士)와 인인(仁人)은 살길을 찾아 인(仁)을 해침이 없고, 자기(自己) 몸을 희생(犧牲)해 인(仁)을 이룸이니라."

시(詩)는 1인칭 즉 가장 개인적 언어로 개인의 독백이 보여주는 서정적 자화상이다. 이는 시라는 작은 그릇에 윤리적으로 모든 덕(德)의 기초(基礎)가 되는 심적(心的) 상태(狀態)에서 많은 뜻과 느낌을 담을 수 있다는 데 그 의의가 있으며 극기복례를 통해 시의 참맛을 낼 수 있으리라는 생각을 한다.

시작(詩作)의 일반화경향을 의식하여 시어와 문체에도 조금씩 변화를 주었다. 앞으로도 문화인들과 서정시의 교류, 문학창달의 궁극적 정신을 통해 서로 다른 인생 이야깃거리를 나누며 적절한 시어들로 여기 한 권의 영역시집을 다듬는다. 늘 따뜻한 마음으로 도움을 준 청향(淸香) 편집장과 친지, 이웃에게 감사드립니다. 나의 작품 편린들을 만나는 존경하는 독자님들께 건강과 축복이 늘 함께하시기를 기원합니다. 아울러 청계문학 회원 여러분의 건승(健勝)과 문운을 빕니다.

2020년 3월 청계서재(淸溪書齋)에서

자정(紫井) 장현경(張鉉景) 삼가 씀

시선(詩仙)과 한적(閑適)

시인이 가는 한적

욕망에 얽매이지 않고
무념무상으로
한적을 추구한다

깊은 수면
강렬한 스트레칭
맛있는 음식과
가볍게 대작하니

유유자적(悠悠自適)
삶 꽃도 피네!

Poetic Genius and Quiet

The quiet of the poet

Without being bound by desire
In a freedom from all ideas and thoughts
Pursue the quiet

Deep sleep
Intense stretching
Delicious food
lightly treated

Deliberately
Life blossoms!

contents

제1부 별이 빛나는 밤에

제2부 회룡포의 봄

제3부 플라멩코

제4부 오사카 기행-자연재해 백화점

제5부 사랑은 영원히

제1부

별이 빛나는 밤에

문장(文章)을 재깔거리게 하라
사상(思想)의 옷을 입혀라
울부짖게 하라!

빨간 채송화(菜松花)

힘겨운 세상살이
하얗게
씻어내고자

가까이 보면
열리는 이 마음

그 속에 감추어진
행복, 슬픈 이야기

여우비 소리 없이
계절을 바꾸듯

비 온 뒤 바람결처럼
깨끗해진 세상

언제나
붉게 피어나
땡볕을 견딘다.

Red Rose Moss

A tough world
Whitely
To wash it off

At close range
This open mind

Hidden in it
Happiness, Sad Story

Without the sound of a sun shower
Season-changingly

Like a wind after rain
A clean world

Always
Red-floating
I endure the sun.

문학이란?

감동적인 언어로
부르짖는
육체(肉體)의 소리다

있는 그대로
쓰는 것은
문학이 아니다

사랑하고, 기뻐하고, 미워하고

그런 삶의 고뇌(苦惱)에서
생산된 꽃이다

문장(文章)을 재깔거리게 하라
사상(思想)의 옷을 입혀라
울부짖게 하라!

Literature?

In a touching language
Cry out
It is the sound of the body

As it is
Writing
Not literature

Love, joy, hate.

In the agony of such a life
It is a flower produced

Let the sentence (written) sneer
Apply the clothes of thought.
Let him cry!

사랑해요!

이 얼마나 아름다운 말인가
또 얼마나 하기 어려운 말인가

사랑하고 사랑받는
내 인생
그런 사람들로 둘러싸인
나의 삶

산다는 것은
사랑하는 일의 연속
사랑하기 때문에
아파하고 눈물 흘린다

사랑할 용기가 없다면
삶은 허망하고
존립하기 어려워
글로나마 연습해 본다

사랑해요!
가족 이웃 그리고 여러분!

I Love You!

What a beautiful words
How hard is that to say?

Loved and loved
My life
Surrounded by such people
My life

Living is
A continuation of love
Because I love you
It hurts and tears come out

If you have no courage to love
Life is a waste
It's hard to survive
Try to practice in writings

I love you!
Family neighbors and everyone!

사랑의 햇빛

기쁘지 아니한가

봄이 오고
여름이 가고
가을이 되어

가진 자도 덜 가진 자도
공수래공수거(空手來空手去)

엄동설한(嚴冬雪寒) 지나
햇빛으로 다시
그 평등한 시작

아, 사랑의 햇빛!

The Sun of Love

I'm very pleased

Spring comes
Summer is over
In autumn

The person who has the person who has less
Comes with empty hands and later goes with empty hands

After the cold
In the sun again
The equal beginning

Oh, the sun of love!

돌 보기를 금같이 하라

지금
자신이

금같이
귀한 시간 속에서
허우적대며

금 보기를
돌같이 하는 것은
아닌지….

Make a Stone Look Gold

Now
In person

like gold
In a precious time
In a fuss

A golden look
What's stoney
I don't know.

웃음꽃

3살쯤의 사내아이가
외발자전거를
타고 가다가

차가 다니는
위험한 골목길에서

갑자기
멈칫하며

마주 오는 어른한테
순간
순수하게 활짝
미소 지으며

"안녕하세요!"

그때
지은 미소는
나에게 던져진
최고의 감탄사!

A Laughing Flower

A boy about three years old
I'm gonna need a single-footed bike
On the ride

Car-riding
In a dangerous alley

Suddenly
With a pause

I'm gonna tell the grown-up
Moment
Purely wide
Smilingly

"Hi!"

Then
The smile you made
Thrown at me
The best exclamation!

그대와 나

봄바람 살랑살랑
초록 빛깔을 흘리며
내 가슴 활짝 연다

봄바람이 포근히
꽃망울을 가득 싣고 와
온 세상을 웃음꽃으로

그리움이 가득한 봄바람은
사랑 가득 안고 와
춤을 춘다

삶이 지칠 때 다가가고 싶은
그대는 봄날의 꽃바람
나 그대를 사랑하리!

You and I

Spring breeze salang salang
In green
I open my heart wide

With a warm spring breeze
Bring a full flower roll
With a smile all over the world

The spring breeze, full of longing
Come with love in your arms
Dance

I want to get closer to life when I'm tired
You are the wind of spring
I will love you!

달빛으로 피는 박꽃

여름이 오는 길목에
달빛 머금고 피어나는
다소곳한 자태

살포시 눈을 뜨며
초가지붕에 몰래
하얀 웃음으로
수줍게 피네

낮보다 밤이 좋아
서린 꿈 묻어놓고
영원으로 피어오르네

무슨 사연 있어
밤이 이슥하도록
달의 정기(精氣) 그리며
달빛과 속살거리나!

Moonlit Gourd Flower

On the way to summer
Moonlit and blooming
A somewhat unsettled figure

With eyes open when sprayed
On a super-graft
With a white laugh
Shyly blooming

I like the night better than the day
With a frosty dream
It's blooming into eternity

What's the story?
The night is so great
Missing the essence of the moon
Moonlight and whisper!

엄마와 딸

닮은 듯하면서 다르고
다른 듯하면서 닮은꼴
둘은 그냥 모녀지간

서로 닮아 싫어하고
너무 같아 품어 안고

울 엄마 손톱이 닳도록 일하고
딸은 손톱을 예쁘게 다듬고

엄마는 딸 생각만
딸은 본인 생각만

엄마가 못다 이룬 꿈
딸이 이뤄주기를
딸은 엄마가 이룬 꿈
내려주기를

서로 끝이 안 보여
엇갈리는 사이
그리워하는 사이

서로 자연으로 돌아가
그 평등한 최후를 맞는다.

Mother and Daughter

It looks like it, but it's different
A different and resemblance
They are a mother and daughter

They don't like each other
I'm so sorry, I'm holding you

My mother works her nails out
She's got a pretty nail

Mom just thought about her daughter
She thinks only about herself

A dream my mother couldn't achieve
I'm not gonna let my daughter
The daughter is a dream
Download

I can't see the end of each other
Intercrossing
In the longing

Back to nature
It is the equal end.

별이 빛나는 밤에

일찍이
광산촌에서 평신도 설교자로
헐벗고 굶주리는 광부들과
차가운 냉방에서 함께하고

스스로는
이웃의 신임과 사랑을 받으며
고뇌한다

종교 없이
신앙을 가슴에 품고
그린 그림에
반짝이는 따뜻한 시선과 빛

고난의 삶 속에서 보이는
크고 힘차며
밝게 빛나는 별

산기슭 집들의 창가에는
따뜻한 사랑이 흐르고
은총이 가득한 밤하늘에는
노란색 별이 수없이 빛나네.

On a Starry Night

Early
A lay preacher in a mining village
Naked and hungry miners
In cold air conditioning

For oneself
With the trust and love of the neighbors
Be agonized

Without religion
With faith in his heart
In a painting
A gleaming warm gaze and light

The life of suffering
Big and powerful
A bright star

The windows of the houses at the foot of the mountain
Warm love flows
In the night sky full of grace
Yellow stars shine a lot.

시(詩)

시는 곧 삶
땀을 흘리는 사람이
쓰는 진실

길을 찾지 못해
헤매던 미로 저 끝에서
나를 끌어당기는 빛

시는 내 생각이
방울방울 맺혀 떨어지는
영롱한 아침 이슬

밤을 새워
새벽을 잉태하는 별

시는 임을 생각하며
다시 써도
이르지 못하는 아픔

내 마음을 밝히는
꺼지지 않는 등불.

Poem

Poetry is life
A sweaty man
Writing truth

I can't find my way
The labyrinth that was wandering
The light that draws me

The poem is about
Droplet-dropping
A brilliant morning dew

All night long
A star that conceives dawn

The thought of poetry
Rewrite
An inexplicable pain

Admonishing my heart
A light that doesn't turn off.

열대야(熱帶夜)

한낮의 태양이
열기만 남아 밤을 태운다

에어컨이나 선풍기로도
자다가 깨고

냉동실 얼음팩으로도
자다가 깨고

찬물로 샤워를 하면
또 하고 싶고

더위와 맞서다가
잠이 안 와 뒤척이던 밤

매미 소리가 한여름 밤을
가쁘게 가르고 있다.

Tropical Night

The midday sun
The heat is only left to burn the night

To air-conditioner or the electric fan
In bed and waking up

With the freezer ice pack
In bed and waking up

When you take a cold shower
I want to do it again

Face the heat
The night I couldn't sleep and turned around

The cicadas were playing in the middle of summer night
Be cut off quickly.

장현경 시집

달빛으로 피는 박꽃

제2부

회룡포의 봄

뿅뿅다리 보일 듯 말 듯
옥빛 시냇물 파란 하늘
금빛 백사장 반짝반짝
강바람 살랑살랑 즐거운 새소리

내 고향은

언제 가 봐도
푸른 공기가 향긋한 고향

순간적으로 떠오르는
고향의 정취 그리며

지그시 눈 감고
그렇게 한참을
향수에 젖다 보면
천지가 내 고향이네!

세월이 흘러도

고향산천에
파란 기다림 뿌리고

수정 같은 밀어로
속삭이면은

고향의 향수는
내 마음속에 오래오래
풋풋한 정으로 자라나리.

My Hometown

When do you go?
A home of fragrant blue air

Instantaneously emerging
In the mood of home

With your eyes closed
For so long
When you get wet with perfume
The world is my home!

Over time

In the mountains of home
With a blue wait

With a crystal whispers
Narrating

The perfume of home is
It's been a long time in my mind
I shall grow up with a good heart.

내 고향은
- 문경 새재

새재의 옛 터전에는
역사극 촬영이 빈번하고
관문에는 지키는 이 없네!

청운의 꿈을 품은 사람들
달빛과 별빛을 등불 삼아
고개를 넘나들었을
높고 험한 문경새재

수많은 선비의 흔적이
새겨진 장원급제길

약수터에서 감로수로
갈증과 피로를 풀고

산수 경관이 수려한 주막에서
한 잔의 술로
세월을 읊네!

여기저기에 새겨진 시비
큰 바위와 작은 바위
나무에도 온통 시

예나 지금이나
시인 묵객들
시상에 잠겨
과거시험 보러 가는 듯
발걸음도 가볍네!

My Hometown
– Mungyeong bird's pass

In the old place of the bird's pass
He's frequently shooting historical plays
There is no guard at the gate!

People who dream of new growth
With moonlight and starlight
I crossed this pass
High and rough Mungyeong bird's pass

There are numerous traces of scholar
The road of top system engraved

From the water supply field to the nectar
I'm thirsty and tired

In the beautiful main floor
A drink
You're reciting the years!

A monument engraved here and there
Large rocks and small rocks
All over the trees

In the past or now
Poets and brushed-up person
In poetic thalamus
As if you were going to take a recruitment test
You're light on your feet!

내 고향은

– 문경 오미자(五味子)

그대 명성
온 세상에 드러내다
수려한 삶터
생동하는 문경
가는 곳이 명산이요
닿는 곳이 명경이라

풍요로운 산간 지역
맑은 물에 키운 생명
청정 계곡에 서린 전설
관민이 품은 넉넉한 인정

곳곳에 오미자 꿈
뜨겁게 자라나고
즐거움 속에
익어가는 빨간 열매
온종일 떠오른다
문경 오미자 산업 특구

붉게 빛나는
오미자 김치에
오미자 빈대떡에
오미자 막걸리에
오미자 동동주.

My Hometown
- Mungyeong Omija

Your reputation
Reveal to the whole world
A beautiful living place
Vibrant Mungyeong
I'm going to famous mountain
It's a great place to reach

Affluent mountainous region
Life raised in clear water
A legend in a clean valley
The generous recognition of the people

Omija dreams all over
Growing hot
In pleasure
Ripe red fruit
Come to mind all day
Mungyeong omija industrial special zone

Red-lighted
Omija kimchi
Omija bean-dae-duck
Omija makgeolli
Omija Dongdongju.

내 고향은
- 조령원(鳥嶺院)

주흘관을 지나니
솔밭과 잣나무
더욱 푸른빛을 발하고
청초한 자태는 솔바람 향기에
신록의 빛 더 눈부시구나

천혜의 조령산과 장엄한 주흘산을
배경으로
병풍을 두른 듯
쌓은 돌 성곽

석문을 지나
고풍 어린 초가집
허물어져 가는 평상에 앉으니

햇살에 비친
온갖 나뭇잎
지난 세월이
못 내 아쉬운 듯
바람 따라 하늘거린다

물건도 교환하고
요기도 할 겸
하룻밤 묵어가려니
보부상들의 옛 얘기
귓전에 맴돈다.

My Hometown
− Cho Ryeong-Won

I passed through the main hall
Pine and pine tree
With a bluer glow
The neat figure is the scent of the pine wind
The light of the green is more dazzling

The Great Choryeong mountain and the magnificent
Juh-hul mountain
In the background
Like a screen
A stone fortress

Through the stone gate
An old-fashioned house
I'm sitting on a crumbling table

Sunlit
All kinds of leaves
Past yearsI feel sorry for you
The wind is flying

We'll exchange things
To eat
I'm going to stay overnight
The old stories of the peddlers
I'm in my ear.

내 고향은
- 회룡포의 봄

낙동강 상류 내성천 지나
솔 향기 가득한 비룡산 계곡
휘감아 돌며
산들바람에 옷깃을 여미고
장안사 올라 보니

수려한 산천
아름다운 우리 강산
사방에 새싹 파릇파릇
산속 여기저기
진달래꽃 살구꽃…
봄의 운치를 더하네!

미륵부처 참배하고
팔각정 회룡대에 올라
천지를 바라보니
회룡포가 무릉도원이라

뿅뿅다리 보일 듯 말 듯
옥빛 시냇물 파란 하늘
금빛 백사장 반짝반짝
강바람 살랑살랑 즐거운 새소리

아! 옛 시인의 시 읊는 소리
들리는 듯하구나.

My Hometown
− Spring of Hoeryongpo

Upstream of The Nakdong River passing by Naesung
Stream
The Mt. Biryong valley full of pine scent
In a circle
With a collar in the breeze
We went up to Jang'an temple

A superb mountain stream
Our beautiful rivers and mountains
All over new bud blue and blue
In the mountains
Azalea apricot⋯
Add to the spring elegance!

To visit the Mireuk Buddha
In the Palgakjeong Hoeryongdae
I look at the heavens and earth
Hoeryongpo is a Utopia

As if it were visible a Pongpong bridge
A jade stream blue sky
A golden white sandy glitter
River wind, pleasant bird sound

Ah! The sound of the old poet's poetry
You sound like you can hear me.

내 고향은
– 대승사와 윤필암

허전한 마음 채우러 떠나는
유서 깊은 불교 성지 대승사

노송이 울창한
사불산 숲길 따라가니

주변 음식점 전혀 없고
산수의 경치 맑아

산간 마을의 정겨운 풍치
산새 소리 바람 타고
수행도량 만나네!

우부도를 돌아
장군수에서 약수 마시고
윤필암에 올라
사불암도 바라보고

대승사 일주문 지나니
고색창연한 절 분위기
형언할 수 없네!

보현암과 묘적암을 그리며
'무(無)라!' 하는 외침이
대승 선원의 고요 속에
들리는 듯하구나!

My Hometown
– Daeseung temple and Yunpilam

Leaving to fill a empty mind
A historic Buddhist holy place

The old pine trees is forested
I follow the forest path of Mt. Sabul

There's no restaurant around
The landscape of mountain and stream is clear

The delightful landscape of a mountain village
In the wind of the mountain birds
You're meeting your performance!

Around Ubudo
Drink some water in the Jangkoonsu
On the yunpilam
I look at the sabulam

Pass the Daeseung temple Iljoo gate
A high-colored temple atmosphere
I can't say!

Missing bohyeonam and maujeogam
The cry of 'nothing!'
In the silence of the Daeseung temple
I can hear you!

내 고향은
– 화장찰해도

어두컴컴한 세상
수행 정진하고
또 참선하여마음의 눈을 뜨니
마음의 귀도 열려

일체 만법이 불생불멸 그대로
삼라만상 일체가 다
무량아승지겁 전부터
미래겁이 다하도록
무진법문 설하는 것을
들을 수 있고
무량불사 하는 것을
볼 수가 있네!

과욕을 삼가고
신경질에 속지 말고
사소취대(捨小取大)하여
지혜롭게 세상을 보면
대해탈이 눈앞에 오는 듯

이 땅은
영원불멸의 빛과 진리로 가득한
용문사 화장찰해도(華藏刹海圖)

세상 어디든
불국토 아닌 곳이 없네!

My Hometown
– Lotus World Drawing

A dark world
In order to performance and devotion
And then practice Zen meditation
Open the eyes of the mind
The ears of the heart are open

All laws are immortality as it is
All of the world
From infinite years ago
To end the time of the distant future
To explaining the Buddhist scriptures
I can hear them
Informing the immortality
I can see it!

With no over-abuse
Don't be fooled by the nerves
Throw away the little and get drunk on the big
If we see the world wisely
It's like a great devolution is coming.

This land
Full of eternal light and truth
Yongmun temple Lotus world drawing

Anywhere in the world
There is no place other than the land of Buddha!

내 고향은
- 김룡사

저 고즈넉한 산사에
누가 머물고 있을까?

아름다운 사계절
아늑하게 들어앉은
김룡사는 어떤 모습일까?

기도 중인 여승들의 근황이 궁금하다
무슨 연유로 비구니가 되었을까?

기품 있고 고요한 사찰에 반했을까?
영혼이 행복하다고 생각했을까?
극락세계로 가려 함일까?
막연히 내세를 위함일까?

이승과 저승을 넘나들며
오늘도 깊숙이
온몸으로 불공드린다.

My Hometown
– Kimryong temple

That quiet mountain temple
Who was staying?

Beautiful four seasons
Cozy-grafted
What is Kimryong temple appearance?

I wonder the current status of the female monks in prayer
What was the reason for Buddhist nun?

Had she been in love with the elegant and still temples?
Did she think her soul was happy?
To the paradise world?
Is it vaguely for the afterlife?

And the world and the world
Deep into the day
I'm going to pray all over.

내 고향은
- 월남막장

사지(死地)에서
생(生)으로의 무사 귀환을 그리며
시린 가슴으로
땅속 깊숙이
컴컴한 굴속으로 내려간다.

갱도 천장을 파란 하늘로 이고
도시락과 고독을 언제나 들고 다니는
막장 인생

탄가루가 흩날리고
무더위에 질식할 듯한 습기
갑자기 '땅! 따! 딴!'
돌이 우는소리도 들으며
컴컴한 굴속에서 굴진 작업하는
이빨만 하얀 칠흑 같은
어둠 속의 흑인
지옥 같은 8시간의 고생대 세계

램프 불에 희미한 월남 막장
갱목은 젖어들고
밤새워 불 밝히며
검붉은 열정으로
석탄을 캐는
진폐증이 머무는 내 몸에

태양은 아득히
저 멀리서 기다린다.

My Hometown
− a Blind End in the Shaft

In the place of death
In the hope of returning to life
With a sore chest
Deep into the ground
I go down into the dark den.

I'm gonna put the shaft ceiling to the blue sky
I'm always carrying lunch boxes and solitude
A desperate life

The coal dust is scattering
A suffocating moisture in the heat
Suddenly, 'Tang! Ta! Tan!'
With the sound of stones crying
Working in a dark den
A white-toothed, pitch-black
Black in the dark
The hellish eight-hour world of Paleozoic

A faint lamplight in a blind end in the shaft
A wooden columns supporting a shaft are wet
All night, lighting up
With a black-red passion
Coal-digging
Pneumoconiosis stays in my body

The sun is far from here
Wait far away.

내 고향은
– 초간정(草澗亭)

졸졸 졸
시냇물 소리가
그윽하게 들리고
고풍 어린 소나무 숲이
바위와 어우러져
그 모습 드러내는
조선시대의 초간정사

널따란 평야에서
부는 바람 소리
용문산 자락에서
들리는 새소리

자연 속에 친화적으로
밀접하게 자리 잡은
초간정의 사계(四季)

책 읽는 소리
낭랑하고 글 쓰는 운치
자연에 묻혀

삶의 지혜와 역사가
더더욱 번쩍거리네!

My Hometown
– Chogan Pavilion

Solzole
The sound of a stream
In a deep voice
The old-fashioned pine forest
In harmony with rock
In the form of
Choganjeongsa in the Joseon Dynasty

In a vast plain
A swelling wind
At the foot of Mt. Yongmun
A sounding bird

Affinity in nature
Closely placed
Four Seasons of Chogan Pavilion

A sound of reading
In a bright and written elegance
Buried in nature

Wisdom and historian of life
It's even more shiny!

내 고향은
- 용문사 윤장대

용문사를 향해 달리다 보면
시간 속으로 빨려 들어가는 듯
예전 우리의 고향 모습이
아득히 떠오른다

허리 구부려 인사하는 천하대장군에
미소 보내고
일주문 지나
천 년 묵은 은행나무에서
그윽이 풍기는 역사 그리며

대장전(大藏殿) 윤장대에서
두 손 모아 합장한다

소원문을 넣고
한 바퀴 돌려 법문을 익히고
두 바퀴 돌려 참을 구하고
세 바퀴 돌려 대해탈을 성취하니

영원한 침묵의 설법
가슴에 가득 담긴 듯

눈이 반짝반짝 빛나고
얼굴도 환하게 웃음 짓는다.

My Hometown
– Yoonjangdae of Yongmun Temple

I'm running towards Yongmun temple
As if it were being sucked into time
To our hometown landscape in the past
Come to mind

To a grand master of bowing back
Smile and
pass the Iljoo gate
A thousand years old ginkgo tree
Researching In the history of the past

In the Yoonjangdae of the Daejangjeon
Put your hands together

With a wish statement
I'm gonna turn around and learn the law
You're gonna have to turn two laps
You've got three laps to get off

The eternal sermon of silence
As if it were full of heart

With a sparkle of eyes
His face smiles brightly.

내 고향은
— 장안사(長安寺)

감입곡류(嵌入曲流) 하는 낙동강에
내성천이 휘돌아
천상의 정기 서린 곳에
비룡(飛龍)이 꿈틀거리고

신라 시대 학이 춤을 추듯
구름이 둥둥
뭇 봉우리가 힘차게 굽이치는 곳에
가람(伽藍)이 서려 있네

신라가 삼국을 통일한 뒤
국태민안을 염원하여 세운
인재의 고을, 용궁 고찰(古刹)

감인세계(堪忍世界)의 번뇌를
잠시 벗어두고
천 년의 소리에
귀 기울이며
다시 찾고 싶은 장안사(長安寺).

My Hometown
− Jhangan Temple

In the Nakdong river which bends and flows
The Naesung stream swings
In the regular aura of heaven
The dragon wriggles

As if the crane dances in the Silla Dynasty
The clouds are floating
where the peaks are bent vigorously
There's a temple standing

After Silla unified the Three Kingdoms
constructing up In the hope of the national security
The village of the talent and the old temple of Yongkung

The agonizing of human world
I'll leave it off for a while
At the sound of a thousand years
With a listen
Jhangan temple which I want to find again.

내 고향은
– 삼강 주막을 찾아

칠백 리 낙동강 물길이
내성천 금천과 만나 어우러지는 여기
삼강 주막 회화나무 아래에 앉아

구성진 뱃노래 소리에
막걸리 몇 잔 머금으니
취기에 옛 정취가 아득히 떠오른다

추억으로 남은 현대식 주막엔
소몰이꾼과 보부상 대신
자동차 물결이 넘실거리네

드센 뱃사람과 장사꾼 시인 묵객들을
밤낮으로 거두어가며 여민
주모의 삼강 주막 오랜 자리 지킴은

정짓간 바람벽에 새긴
술어미의 칼금 벽화를
한과 연민의 예술로 승화하고

하풍 나루 회룡포 용포 나루로
이어지는 뱃길을 열어
나룻배가 띄워지리라

몸과 마음은
시대의 변화에 춤을 추고
배추전과 막걸리의 우리네 정서는
시간과 역사의 격랑 속에서도

삼강 주막은
오래오래
살아 숨 쉬리라.

My Hometown
– Find the Samgang Tavern

700ri Nakdong River Road
Here, where you meet and mingle with Geum stream in
Naeseong stream
Sitting under pictorial tree in the Samgang tavern

In the composed boat song
I've got a few makgeolli
The old mood comes to mind in the drunken days

The modern tavern left in memory
Instead of the cowboy and peddler
The car's waving

The coarse boat man and peddler, poets
Day and night and reaping
The mother's long-standing position at the Samgang tavern

Inscribed on the wind wall
The sword-and-gold murals of the wine mother
Sublimating into the art of compassion and the resentment

To Hapung Naru Hoeryongpo Yongpo Naru
Open the ensuing waterway
The ferry will float

Body and mind
Dancing in the changes of the times
Our sentiments of cabbage swelling and makgeolli
In the midst of the turbulence of time and history

The Samgang tavern
Long time
It'll breathe alive.

내 고향은
- 산택연꽃공원

충효의 고장 예천
물 맑고 인정 많은 용궁
고즈넉한 산택 마을에
우뚝 선 고종산

그 아래
불교와 유교가 융성하던 시대에
삼다사상 기운으로
탄생한 산택지(山澤池) 연꽃

자생수 연못에 만발한
자생 연꽃의 향연
연못을 뒤덮는
수많은 연잎의 물결

하늘빛 어우러진 연못 위로
수채화처럼 흩뿌려진 연꽃 향기에
지나는 길손걸음을 멈추네!

넓은 잔디 광장
산철쭉 수양버들 야생화는
진녹색의 둥근 연잎
더 푸르게 하고

성자의 꽃, 부활의 꽃이 어리는
인근 휴양지의 중심
산택 연꽃공원
그 자취 영원하여라
그 향기 영원하리라.

My Hometown
– Santaek Lotus Park

The Yecheon town of loyalty and filial piety
A clear and acknowledging in Yongkung
In a quiet Santaek village
High-rise Mt. Kojong

Under it
In the days of Buddhism and Confucianism
In the spirit of the thought of three
A mountain and pond born lotus flower

In full bloom in the self-made pond
A feast of native lotus
Pond-covering
The wave of a great deal of lotus foliage

Over a sky-blue pond
In the lotus scent scattered like the watercolor
Passing vagabond
Stop walking!

A wide grass square
The azalea, water-cultivated willows, wildflower
A dark green round lotus leaves
Greener and greener

The flowers of the saints, the flowers of resurrection
The center of a nearby resort
Santaek lotus park
Be eternal in your tracks
The scent will last forever.

장현경 시집

달빛으로 피는 박꽃

제3부
플라멩코

삶의 기쁨과 괴로움
사랑과 미움
애수와 정열이 담겨 있네!

병마용갱(兵馬俑坑)

거대한 대륙
전설 같은 이야기
2,200여 년 전
그 옛날을 그려 봐

흙으로 빚어 구운
병사와 군신병마(君臣兵馬)

진시황 사후에도
수호신(守護神)으로
금세 뛰어나올 것 같은
마부와 궁수의 기세

피가 흐르는 듯
지상 세계로 걸어 나온
호위무사(護衛武士)들의 함성
소리 없이 들려 와

오늘도
진시황제를 지키고 있네!

The Soldier and Horse in The Grave

A great continent
A legendary story
2,200 years ago
Picture the old days

Soil-baked
Military Soldiers and vassals

Even after the death of the Emperor Jinxi
By the guardian god
Like a rush
The spirit of the horseman and archer

Like blood is flowing
Walking out into the world
The shouts of escort warriors
It's heard silently

Today
You're guarding the Emperor Jinxi.

양귀비화

언제부터인가
붉은 선혈로
들길을 밝히는
향기로운 양귀비화(楊貴妃花)

양귀비는 본래
당 현종의 귀비로
세속의 꽃들을 비웃겠노라

한들거리는 붉은 꽃을
찌는 듯 무더위가 가슴을 조여와도
관능적인 몸매와 유혹의 얼굴이
만 가지 자태로 나타나
장엄하게 피워낸 경국지색(傾國之色)

꽃들의 향연으로
모든 근심 사라져
여기저기 우후죽순
애틋한 몸짓에

옛 시인의 시 읊는 소리
꽃잎 위에 붉게 모여
백발이 다 되도록
서럽게 전하고 있네!

Poppy Flower

Since when?
To blood
Making bright to field road
Scentful poppy flower

poppy was originally
As a noble queen of the Tang Dynasty
I will laugh at the flowers of the world

To a shimmering red flower
The heat of the heat has tightened my chest
The sensual body and the face of temptation
In 10,000 different shapes expressively
The extremes of beauty that have been majesticly created

With the feast of flowers
All your worries go away
All over the place
In a tender gesture

The recital of an old poet
Being Congregated to Red on the petals
So that the white hair is done
I'm telling you something.

플라멩코

춤은 육체로 쓰는 가장 아름다운 시(詩)
빈손으로 표현할 수 있는 가장 큰 외침

춤과 발 구르며
내는 소리와 손뼉 소리
기타반주와 슬픈 노래에는

삶의 기쁨과 괴로움
사랑과 미움
애수와 정열이 담겨 있네!

어둠에서 불길이
갑자기 솟아오르는 것 같은 정열
신들린 사람처럼 춤을 추는 몸놀림
구원을 갈구하는 듯한 애절한 노랫소리
기타의 환상적인 음률

집시의 여왕
카르멘의 무대가 아니더라도

플라멩코 무대에서
있는 그대로
타오르는 태양처럼
그들과 섞여
강렬한 춤을 추고 싶다
그들과 섞여
불처럼 타오르고 싶다.

Flamenco

Dance is the most beautiful poem written by the body
The loudest cry to be expressed empty-handed

Dancing and rolling feet
The sound of hand and hand
The guitar accompaniment and the sad song

Joy and suffering in life
Love and hate
It's a grief and a passion!

In the dark, the flames
A sudden rising passion
Dancing like a godly person
A sad song that seemed to crave salvation
The fantastic tone of the guitar

Queen of gypsy
If it's not Carmen's stage

On the flamenco stage
As it is
Like a burning sun
Mixed with them
I want to dance intensely
Mixed with them
I want to burn like a fire.

하롱베이 선상에서

비릿한 바다 냄새
푸르고 깊은 고요의 바다 위에
드리워져 있는 안개비

석회암의 기암절벽과 그 그림자
경이로운 천상의 동굴
다도해의 아름다움
그대로 간직한 채
태초의 모습
풍화의 숨결로 가다듬는다

바위산들이 병풍처럼 둘러싸여
섬 사이를 유유히 지나가는 유람선
선상에서 맛보는
월남의 전통주와 생선회
복잡한 인간세계 잠시 잊고
신선의 세계에 들어선 듯한
착각에 빠져본다

가는 길
오는 길
작은 쪽배에 삶을 의지한 채
열대 과일을 하나 더 팔려는
어린 소녀의 모습이
어른거린다.

On the Harong Bay Line

A bleak sea smell
On the blue, deep, still sea
A drizzled mist

The Rock Cleaves of Limestone and Their Shadows
A marvelous heavenly cave
Beauty of many islands
With the scenery
The appearance of the beginning of the world
Clear with the breath of weathering

The rocky mountains are surrounded by folding screens
A cruise ship that passes through the islands
Tasting on a ship
Traditional Wine and Sashimi in Vietnam
For a moment, forget the complicated human world
As if it were a fresh world
All into an illusion

A path to go
A path to come here
With my life on a small boat
Sale by one more the tropical fruit
The image of a little girl
Glimmering in front of my eyes.

알혼섬

민족의 시원(始原)에서
잊힌 문화 찾으러
러시아의 시베리아 남쪽에 있는
풍요로운 호수 바이칼호로
길을 낸다

이르쿠츠크 동쪽에 있는 호수로
크기는 경상도와 비슷하며
세계에서 7번째로 큰 호수이자
수심이 깊고 부피는
5대호와 비슷하다

민물호수에 수심 40m까지
내려다보일 만큼 투명하여
명명된 '시베리아의 푸른 눈'

바이칼 호수 내의 유인도인
알혼섬에는
다양한 전설이 서식하고 있다.

Alhon Island

In the origin of the nation
To find a forgotten culture
In the south of Siberia
Affluent lake baikal
Make a way

To the lake east of Irkutsk
The size is similar to the kyungsangdo in Korea
The seventh largest lake in the world
Deep water and volume
It is similar to the 5 Great Lake

Freshwater lake to 40 meters deep
In a clear enough way to look down
The named 'Blue Eyes of Siberia'

The manned island within Lake Baikal
Alhon Island
Various legends are inhabited.

게르

몽골인들의 안락한
보금자리

넓은 초원 위에
타원형으로 여기저기
이동하는 집
게르(Ger)

나무와 버들가지로
벽을 만들고
그 위에
양털로 만든 펠트로
덮어씌운다

오랜 세월
몽골인들은
아늑한 천막집으로
드넓은 초원을
누비고 다니네.

Ger

The comfort of the Mongols
Nesting place

On a large meadow
Elliptical here and there
Moving house
Ger

With trees and willow branches
To build a wall
On top of it
Wool felts
Overlay

Long years
Mongols
In a cozy tent
A vast meadow
You're walking around.

한궈 마을

어떤 동네에
베트남 처녀 10에 8은
한국으로 시집가네

한국 총각
친절하고 잘살아서
인기가 최고

시집가면 부자가 된 듯
덩달아 베트남 친정도
부자가 된다

혼자 사는 베트남 노총각

국제결혼에 실패해서
귀국하는 여인을 보면
기뻐할까, 슬퍼할까?

Korean Village

In a neighborhood
Eight in a Vietnamese maiden ten
I'm marrying to Korean man

Korean bachelor
Kind and well-off
The best of popularity

She think she is rich in marriage
So her home in Vietnam
Be rich

A single Vietnamese old bachelor

Failure to marry internationally
If he see the woman who returns Vietnam home
Will he be happy or sad?

베트남 머드 온천

아이 리조트 코스
상쾌한 녹색 공간에 있는
머드 온천

욕장에는 가족처럼 남녀 구분 없이
동호인마다
이야기꽃을 피운다

진흙탕이 옷인 양
부끄럼도 없이
처음 경험하는 듯
키득키득 웃음꽃이 핀다

달걀과 진흙을 테마로
장식한
에그 머드 스파
색다른 즐거움을 주네.

Vietnam Mud Spa

Eye resort course
In the refreshing green space
Mud spa

In the bathtub, like the family, without the distinction
of man and woman
For each club
Make a story

Like a muddy suit
Without shame
As if you've never experienced it
I can't believe I'm laughing

With eggs and mud
Decorating
Egg mud spa
It gives you a different pleasure.

아융강 래프팅

쏴악 흐르는 계곡물 소리가
더욱 크게 들리는 듯

급류 타는 전율과 도전정신
주변의 빼어난 산세가
강물에 반사되어
그림 같은 절경을 뽐내고

고무보트를 타고
심신 계곡의 열대우림을 감상하며
때론 급류와 폭포
여기저기 나타나는 장애물에
부딪혀가며 즐기는
스릴 넘치는 레포츠

하나둘! 하나둘!
노를 저어
바이킹 구령에
보트가 좌우로 심하게 움직여

물세례에 물벼락도 맞고
풍덩 강물에 휩쓸리는
이열치열의 피서
아융강 래프팅.

Ayoong River Rafting

The sound of the ravine water
It sounds even louder

The thrill and spirit of challenge in the rapids
The great mountain around
Reflected in the river
With a picture of the landscape

On a rubber boat
To watch the rainforests of the valleys
Sometimes rapids and falls
In the obstacles that appear here and there
A bumpy, enjoyable
Thrilling leisure

One, two! One, two!
Row
In the Vikings command
Boat moves from side to side badly

The water is struck by the water baptism
A river-colliding
Summer heat fighting heat
Ayoong river rafting.

수상 가옥

저 멀리
넓은 톤레사프 호수 위에
보트를 타고
수상가옥 한 채 지어볼까?

크메르인들과
일상생활을 해보면
어떨까?

낮에는 가끔
청정 하늘에
수묵화를 수놓고
저녁에는
황금빛 일몰에
시를 써 볼까!

한 시간 고기 잡아
연명할 수 있으니

이러다
여행중독증 들면
그동안
글 못 썼던 세월
아까워서 어찌하나!

A House of Water

Far away
On a broad Tonressaf lake
On a boat
Shall we build a house?

The Khmers
You know, I live just daily life
What do you think?

Occasionally during the day
In the clean sky
Embroidered with ink painting
In the evening
At the golden sunset
Let's write a poem!

Take an hour of meat
I can live with it

Do this
Travel addiction
In the meantime
Years of inability to write
What's wrong with you?

앙코르와트

초록 숲의 단아한
열대 우림의 소박한 전원 풍경
아름다운 씨엠립

찬란한 황금 문명
사원의 도읍지
앙코르와트여!

인간의 작품인가!
신의 섭리인가!
웅장하고 우아하고 정교하구나

12세기 캄보디아 전성기에
탄생한 하늘의 궁전 앙코르와트
신화와 전설이 스며 있구나

캄보디아에 우뚝 솟은
밀림사원 앙코르와트
역사의 주인답게
세계 7大 불가사의로
이름을 떨치는구나.

Angkor Wat

The simpleness of the green forest
The simple rural landscape of rainforests
Beautiful Siem Reap

A brilliant golden civilization
The town of the temple
Angkor Wat!

The work of man!
God's offering!
You are magnificent, elegant and sophisticated!

In the 12th century Cambodia
The palace of heaven, Angkor Wat
Myths and legends are permeating

A great rise in Cambodia
A jungle temple called Angkor Wat
As master of history
The Seven Wonders of the World
You're making your name famous.

피피섬

타이 북부지역
세계 10대 관광지
치앙마이

남쪽 푸껫에서 다시 만난 인연
신(神)만이 만들 수 있는 환상의 섬
피피돈 피피레

기암절벽과 에메랄드빛 바다
곱고 흰 산호 해변
잔잔한 파도

수많은 종류의 열대어들이
떼를 이루는 수중세계

원시 자연 속 그대로의 열대 낙원
여유로운 분위기를 물씬 풍기는
야자수 정글

깨끗하고 고운 모래톱
세계에서 가장 아름다운 해변

언제든지 바다에 뛰어들 수 있는
더운 날씨와 수온

고즈넉하고 때 묻지 않은
항상 푸르게 반짝이는 바다.

Pippi Island

Northern thai region
The world's top ten tourist destinations
Chiang Mai

The relationship we met again in the south
The island of fantasy that only God can make
Pipidone pipirre

Rock cliffs and emerald seas
A fine coral beach
A calm wave

A lot of tropical fish
A herd of underwater worlds

Tropical paradise as it is in primitive nature
A relaxed atmosphere
Palm jungle

A clean, fine sandbar
The most beautiful beach in the world

You're a man who can jump into the ocean
Hot weather and water temperature

A quiet, unspoilt
The sea always shines blue.

팍상한 폭포

수평선 따라 곡선으로 달리다
갑자기 마주친 계곡

원주민 사공이 끄는 카누
유유히 노를 젓다가
바닥이 드러난 바위 사이를
끌고 밀고 젓고 발로 차며
힘차게 오른다

깎아지른 듯한 수직 절벽에
달라붙은 열대 밀림들
여기저기 하늘에서 떨어지는
작은 폭포에 땀을 씻고
물보라를 맞으며
역류해 가는 막다피오강

길게 목을 늘어뜨리고 반기는 야자수
사방이 둘러싸여진 절벽 사이로
우물같이 보이는 하늘
천연색 노을 속에 펼쳐지는
천혜의 절경
힘차게 약동하는 뗏목의 그림자

폭풍 속의 비바람처럼
온몸으로 폭포수를 맞는
세계 7대 비경.

Pagsangjan Falls

Run along a horizontal line in a curve
A ravine that I suddenly encountered

A canoe drawn by a native sagong
Paddle gently
Between the rocks that showed the floor
Dragging him, stirring him, kicking him
Rise vigorously

On a shaved vertical cliff
Clinging rainforests
Falling from the sky
I'll wash my sweat in a small waterfall
In a spray
Refluxing makdafio river

A long, hanging palm tree
Between cliffs surrounded by all sides
A well-looking sky
The natural color glow spreads
A grand view
The shadow of a vigorously moving raft

Like the rain and wind in a storm
All over the waterfall
Seven mystery worlds.

어떤 할머니

발리 아융강 래프팅에
이고 진 저 늙은이
생활전선에 나섰다

그것도 오래전
나약한 60대 할머니가 맨발로
하루에도 십여 차례

80여 험한 계단을
한 걸음씩 오르내린다

험한 계곡 래프팅에 뒹굴어 온 고무보트
압축하고 묶어서
물방울이 뚝뚝 뚝
머리에 이고
두 팔로 균형을 잡으며
간신히 허리를 편다

바람이 불면 넘어질 듯
근육이 없어
뼈대만 남은 다리가 부러질까
왠지 불안하여
가까이 갈 수가 없다

파르르 떠는 듯한
그녀의 몸짓
독거노인인가
후손이 있는가
삶이 얼마나 남았다고!

A Grandmother

In the Bali Aoong River rafting
That old woman who was put it on the head
She has set out on the living front

That was a long time ago
A weak, a grandmother in her 60s barefoot
A dozen times a day

80 rough steps
Take a step up and down

Rubber boats rolled over rough valley rafting
Compress and bind
A drip of water
On the head
Balancing with his arms
Barely stretch one's waist

When the wind blows, it falls-like
Muscleless
Is there a broken leg that only left the skeleton?
In some unease
I can't get close

As if floating trembly
Her gesture
The elderly living alone
Are there descendants?
How much life is left!

장현경 시집

달빛으로 피는 박꽃

제4부

오사카 기행 - 자연재해 백화점

쓰나미는
이재민에게 스트레스를
국민에겐 불안감을 증폭시킨다

오사카 기행 1
−고베 대지진

일본에서 6번째 큰 도시
인구 150만 명으로
상업의 중심이며 아름다운
항구 도시인 고베에

1995년 1월 17일 새벽 5시 46분에
경고도 없이
지진이 도시를 흔든다

400년 동안 잠자다가
진도 7.2를 앞세워 20초 만에
고베는 초토화된다

5,502명의 희생자
23만 5천 명이 집을 잃고
10만 채 이상의 건물이 무너졌다
피해액은 1,500억 달러

목재 기둥에 무거운 기와지붕이
지진에 쉽게 무너져
89%가 안타깝게 희생되었다

재앙은 가끔 우연이가 아닌
연속된 사건들의 결과를
따라다닌다.

Osaka Travel 1
- Kobe Earthquake

6th largest city in Japan
With a population of 1.5 million
The center of commerce and beautiful
Port city of Kobe

January 17, 1995, 5:46 a.m.
Without warning
An earthquake shakes the city

I've been sleeping for 400 years
With a magnitude of 7.2 in 20 seconds
Kobe is devastated

5,502 victims
235,000 people lost their homes
More than 100,000 buildings have collapsed
Damage amounted to $150 billion

The roof of tile heavying in the timber post
It easily collapses in the earthquake
89% were sadly sacrificed

Disasters are sometimes not accidental
The consequences of successive events
Disasters are following about event.

오사카 기행 2
- 청수사(淸水寺)에서

오랜 세월 수많은 사람이
이곳의 아름다운 사계를 그리며
건강과 복을 기원한다는
교토의 유서 깊은 물의 사원

좁은 산비탈로 올라가는 길 양쪽에
호화찬란한 간판이 빼곡히 박혀 있고
따가운 햇볕이 늦여름에도
여행객의 등 뒤에 숨어서
이리저리 계속 따라다니니
비 오듯 줄줄 흐르는 땀

층층이 절 마당에 들어서니
고풍스러운 법당을 신형 목탑이
주황색으로 에워싸
햇빛에 번쩍거려 눈이 부신다

인파에 떠밀리며 전망대에 이르니
못질이 전혀 없는 본당의 기둥
무거워 보이는 지붕이
거센 태풍을 끄떡없이 견디어내네

교토 시내를 내려다보며
절벽에서 흐르는 음용수로
손과 입 먼저 씻어내고
'장수 건강 학문'의 이치를 깨달으며
의중(意中)에 품고 있는 소원을 빌었네!

Osaka Travel 2

− At Cheongsoo Temple

A lot of people have been for a long time
In the beautiful four worlds of this place
Wishing for health and blessing
The historic water temple of Kyoto

On both sides of the road to the narrow hillside
With a gorgeous signboard
In the late summer, the sun was so hot
Hiding behind the back of the traveller
You keep following me around
A raining sweat

I was in the yard upstairs
The old-fashioned courthouse is a new wooden tower
Enclosed in orange
The sun flashes and my eyes are gorgeous

And then we're pushed by the crowd
A pillar of a nave with no nails
The roof that looks heavy
It can't help but endure a storm

Overlooking downtown Kyoto
A drinking waterway flowing from a cliff
Wash your hands and mouth first
Realizing the reason of 'longevity, health and learning'
I wished for the wish I had in my mind!

오사카 기행 3
– 인력거

관광하는 사람들
비행기 자동차로 왔다 갔다 하다가
무슨 일로 인력거를 타는가

금테 안경에 여송연을 물고
뉘 집 규수 서방이 되고 싶었는가

관광지에서 보이는 인력거
어름어름 손님을 태워
부드러운 동작에 밝은 표정으로
도란도란 이야기로 길을 내며
요리조리 달린다

자칫하면 넘어져 박힐 듯싶게
휘뚝휘뚝하는 인력거
운전대를 힘껏 잡은 팔뚝
불끈거리는
인력거부(人力車夫)의 맥박 소리

커다란 바퀴가 힘차게 굴러가듯
숨 가쁜 하루가 스쳐 지나간다.

Osaka Travel 3
– Rickshaw

Tourists
Come and go in a plane and car
What are you doing on a rickshaw?

With the cigar in the gold-rimmed glasses
Did you want to be the bridegroom of maiden?

A rickshaw in a tourist area
I'm gonna need you to pick up a guest
With a soft, bright look
In the path of the Dorandoran story
Run on a dish

I'm afraid I'll fall down
A wiggling rickshaw
Forearms that grip the steering wheel
Flailing
The pulse of the refusal of manpower

Like a big wheel rolling vigorously
A breathless day passes.

오사카 기행 4
– 오사카성을 보고

이곳은 낯선 성(城)
단순히
돌로 쌓은 성이 아닌 듯

무언가 두려운 듯
건널 수 없는 호수로
둘러싸인 탄탄한 성곽(城郭)

권력의 상징인 오사카성
그 위에 우뚝 서 있는 천수각

육중한 출입문
그 속에 드나드는 작은 문

바윗돌에 자라나는 검푸른 이끼들
빛바랜 팻말에 새겨진 기도문

오랜 세월 묵묵히 버텨오네!

Osaka Travel 4
– See Osaka Castle

This is a unfamiliar castle
Simply
As if it were not a stone castle

As if he were afraid of something
To the lake that can't be crossed
Surrounded solid castle

Osaka Castle, a symbol of power
A towering angle on it

A heavy door
A small door in and out of it

Dark blue moss growing on the rocks
Prayers engraved on faded signs

Silently holding out for years!

오사카 기행 5
– 쓰레기통이 없다

깨끗하다
관광지나 거리에
휴지 하나
담배꽁초 하나
보이지 않는다

쓰레기는 휴대하여
매점 호텔 집으로
가져간다

자동판매기엔
음료수용 쓰레기통이
있다

거리를 걸어가며
담배 피우는 사람이
없다

다른 사람에게
폐를 끼치지 않는 성향의
극치다.

Osaka Travel 5
– There is no trash can

Be clean
On a tourist attraction or street
A tissue paper
A cigarette butt
Be invisible

The garbage carries with one
At the canteen, hotel, house
Take it

In the vending machine
The trash can for the beverage
There is

Walking down the street
A smoker
No

To the others
A tendency not to cause a nuisance
Be extreme.

오사카 기행 6
- 관광버스

덜 먹고
덜 입고
덜 쓰는 문화가
녹아있는 관광버스

그리 불편하거나
옹색한 모습이 아니면서
환경 보존에
도움이 되네.

Osaka Travel 6
– Tour bus

Less-eating
Underwear
A less-used culture
A permeating tourist bus

It's not that uncomfortable
You're not looking so stiff
To environmental conservation
That helps.

오사카 기행 7
- 수돗물

수돗물을
그대로 마신다

어디서든
당연히 마실 수 있다

변기 덮개는
한여름에도 따뜻하다

손 씻은 물은
변기통으로 간다.

Osaka Travel 7

— Tap water

Tap water
Drink as it is

Anywhere
Of course you can drink

The toilet cover
It is warm in the middle of summer

The water washed by hands
Goes to the toilet.

오사카 기행 8
- 자연재해 백화점

태풍 1호, 태풍 2호
　　태풍 4호

지진 봄, 지진 여름
　　지진 겨울

쓰나미는
이재민에게 스트레스를
국민에겐 불안감을 증폭시킨다

자연재해 대국에서
재해 대처 선진국으로.

Osaka Travel 8
– Department Store for Natural Disasters

Typhoon No. 1, Typhoon No. 2
Typhoon no. 4

Seismic Spring, Seismic Summer
Earthquake winter

A tsunami
The stress to the victims
It amplifies anxiety for the people

In a natural disaster country
To the advanced countries that deal with disasters.

북해도(北海道) 1
– 4월 초(初)

홋카이도(Hokkaido)는 북위 43도
함경북도 종성과 비슷하게 위치하며
우리나라 면적의 83%
인구는 5백 3십여만 명

봄이라고 하지만
날마다 시도 때도 없이
싸락눈이 흩날리고
함박눈이 펄펄 펄
때로는
봄비가 눈과 섞여 내리니
봄 같지 않네

영하 30도 한겨울에도
얼지 않는 시코츠 호수(湖水)
제 생긴 대로 모습을 드러내는
산과 수목들의 그림자가
윤슬과 어우러져
둘레 42km인 호안(湖岸)에는
신비(神秘)의 물결 더해 주는구나

광활한 영토에는
골퍼 천국을 이루고
살찐 말들은 짙푸름 위에
막힘없이 뛰논다.

Hokkaido 1

– Early April

Hokkaido is 43 degrees north latitude
It is located similar to Jongseong in North Hamgyong
Province
83% of the area in Korea
The population is 5.3 million

It's spring, but
At any time every day
A fluttering of hail
With the snowflake
At times
The spring rain is mixed with snow
It's not like spring

In the midwinter of minus 30 degrees
Lake Sikotsu which does not freeze
Showing to shadow-revealing
The shadows of the mountains and trees
In harmony with the high light
The lake, which is 42 km in circumference,
You add to the waves of mysteries

In a vast territory
In the form of a golfer's heaven
The fat horses are on the deep blue
Run without a clogging.

북해도(北海道) 2
– 쇼와신잔(昭和新山)

1943년 12월

보리밭에
지진과 함께
2년 동안 화산활동으로
쇼와시대에 생겨난 화산

402m 높이에
표면 온도 300도
세계 유일한 벨로니테
활화산

용암이 분출하지 못하고
대지가 융기하여 생긴
붉은색 고구마산

지금도 산 곳곳에
연기가 무럭무럭 솟는다.

Hokkaido 2
– Showa Shinzan (New Mountain)

December 1943

In barley field
With earthquake
Two years of volcanic activity
Volcanoes that originated in the Showa period

402m high
Surface temperature 300 degrees
The world's only bellonite
Active volcano

Lava can't erupt
Born to the land's uplift
Red sweet potato mountain

Even now here and there at the mountain
The smoke rises.

북해도 3
– 온천 지옥 계곡

온천의 원수(原水)가 나오는 곳
노보리베츠 지옥 계곡

희뿌연 한 지옥의 분위기
출입금지 팻말
유황 냄새에
잿빛 물이 흐르고

료칸과 온천 거리에
분당 3,000리터씩 공급되는
다양한 종류의 온천수

80도의 뜨거운 온천수가
간헐천으로 분출하여
끓어오르는 수증기 지옥

나무도
풀 한 포기도 없는
붉은 황토색의 지옥 계곡.

Hokkaido 3
– Hot Spring Hell Valley

The place where the raw water of the hot spring comes out
Novoribetz hell valley

A lush atmosphere of hell
No-go sign
In the smell of sulfur
Gray water flows

On the streets of Ryokan and Hot Springs
3,000 liters per minute
Various kinds of hot spring water

80 degrees of hot spring water
Erupt into the geyser
Boiling steam hell

No tree
Without a wad of grass
The red ocher hell valley.

북해도 4
– 도리무시 우동

일본 우동에
국물이 없다

사각형 나무 그릇에
만두 감자 옥수수 닭고기를
섞어
쪄서 먹는 우동

소스에 찍어 먹는다

짜고 달고
담백하여
맛이 나네!

Hokkaido 4

─ Dorimushi Udong

Japanese udong
Have no soup

In a square wooden bowl
Dumpling, potato, corn, chicken
In mixing up
Udong eaten in boiling

Take a sauce

Weaving and sweeting
In a light taste
It tastes good!

북해도 5

- 노천탕

캄캄한 새벽하늘에서
함박눈이 어깨 위로
펄펄 흩날리고
몸은 물에 가라앉아
땀이 뻘뻘

반갑다고
눈 그림을 그리는
앞산에 까마귀

은백색 탕에서 돌계단을 밟고
황금색 탕으로
만병통치인 듯
사람들 탕 치유를 한다

그 옛날 향수를 자극하는
호텔 노천탕
추억을 그린다.

Bukhae Province 5

− Openair bath

In the dark dawn sky
The snowflakes over the shoulder
The snow is blowing
Your body sinks in the water
Sweaty is flowing

Nice to meet you
Snow-drawing
A crow in the front mountain

In a silver-white bath, stepping on a stone staircase
To a golden bath
As if it were a panacea
People heal in the baths

Arousing the old nostalgia
Hotel openair bath
I long for memories.

북해도 6
- 삿포로 테레비 탑

삿포로 TV 탑은
147m 높이의 철탑

어디서나 잘 보여
북해도에서 가장 높은 건물

오도리 공원의 상징

TV 탑 전망대에서 보는
아름다운 삿포로의 밤.

Bukhae Province 6
– Sapporo Terevi Tower

Sapporo TV tower
A 147m high pylon

I can see it everywhere
The tallest building in the Hokkaido

Symbol of Odori park

Beholding at the TV tower observatory
The beautiful night of Sapporo.

장현경 시집

달빛으로 피는 박꽃

제5부

사랑은 영원히

사랑은
이승과 저승을 넘나들며
삶을 영속시킨다

겨울이라기엔 아직

11월이라 하더라도
겨울이라기엔 아직 일러
서로 시소게임 하네

천상에선
밤을 초겨울이라 하고
낮은 초가을이라 하네

그러자
지상에서 다시

누가 더 노랗게 물드나
누가 더 붉게 물드나?

Not Yet for Winter

Even in November
It's not too early for winter
They play seesaw games

In heaven
I'm calling the night early winter
It's called the low early autumn

Then
On the ground again

Who's yellower
Who's redder?

돌개바람

미풍의 속삭임으로
풀잎 사이를 스치다가
순식간에
나뭇잎을 흔들며
한바탕 휘몰아친다

살아있는 것들의
빙빙 도는 숨소리

죽은 듯 떨어지다가
되살아나는
그 끈질긴 목숨.

A Wind of Stone

In a whisper of the breeze
Skim between the grass leaves
In a flash
Waving leaves
Be a little fluttering

The side of living things
A spinning breathing

Fall dead
Resurfacing
That persistent life.

알밤을 담으며

온몸을 가시 옷으로 감싸고
무더운 여름 거쳐
가을바람 부니
성근 가시 곧 세운다

가을 풍경 색색이 물들 때
가시 옷을 훌훌 벗고
힘차게
풀숲으로 낙하한다

욕심을 내거나
조급해하면
가시에 찔려 피가 흐른다

한 알 또 한 알
바구니에 담는 기쁨

사랑스럽다
알밤이.

With Chestnuts in It

Enveloped my whole body around a thorny dress
After a hot summer
Being windy in the autumn
The thorns of the growth are soon to be erected

When the color of the autumn landscape is dyed
With a thorny gown off
Vigorously
Fall into the grass

Either greedy or
If you're impatient
Blood flows from a thorn

Another egg
Joy in a basket

Be lovely
The chestnuts.

어떤 기행(奇行)

숨죽여 살았던 시절이 있었다
때로는 선인장도 살아남기 힘든 사막의 길을 걷고
모래바람에
뿌리까지 말려버리겠다는 듯이
이글거리는 태양으로 멈출 줄 몰라

목이 탈수록 더 많이 땀방울이 흐른다는 것을
보여주려는 듯
스스로 그늘을 만들어
시를 사랑하고 소설을 그리며
어린 영혼을 쉬게 하려는 포석의 문학

두 눈 속에 깊은 열정을 모아
강물을 물들이고
주름진 산등성이를 헤치며 달려온 마흔네 해

흔적을 찾아 불던 바람도
선구자의 발자국 아래 머문다

세월이 흐를수록 흔들리지 않는 지혜
낮은 데로 흐르는 겸손 그리고
젊은이의 혈맥을 찾아

이 나라가 숲으로 이루어진
뼈대 굵은 산맥들로 뻗어 나가게
내일을 떠받치는 조명희 문학관

이 땅이 넓어졌네
이 땅이 더욱 넓어져
눈이 부시게 목마른 영혼을 적시리.

What's Your Travel?

There was a time when I lived under my breath
Sometimes the cactus walks through the desert which is
hard to survive
In the sandy wind
As if they were going to dry up their roots
I can't stop with the blazing sun

The more you get thirsty, the more sweaty you're gonna get
As if to show
Shades themselves
Love poetry, draw novels
A Phoseok literature to rest a young soul

I am so passionate about my eyes
In the river
Forty-four years I've been running through the
corrugated ridge

The wind that was blowing for trace
Stay under the trailblazer's footprint

Wisdom that does not shake as the years pass
A low-flowing humility and
Find the young man's blood

This country is a forest
Spread out into the thick, bone-to-frame mountains
Jo Myung hee Literary Museum to Support Tomorrow

This land has widened
This land is widening
Wet your thirsty soul with a blinding eye.

가을 무정(無情)

건들바람 타고
쑥 올라간 가을 하늘

황금빛으로 일렁이는
평원(平原)

온통 붉게 물들어
선명하게 선을 그리는 산등성이

연못가에 청초하게
피어있는 들국화
그 위를 맴도는 고추잠자리

열려오는 이 가을
아, 내 마음의 창(窓)!

Autumn Heartlessness

In a wind-shattering
A sky of autumn

The Golden light is swaying
Plains

It's all red
A clear line of ridges

Cleanly by the pond
Blooming wild chrysanthemum
A chili dragonfly hovering over it

This coming autumn
Oh, the window of my heart!

약속

아침에 눈을 뜨면
태양이 떠오른다

오늘을 살아갈 일로
두려움과 공허감이 앞선다

반가운 척 웃고
기쁘게 말을 하고
지키지 못할 약속을 하고
누군가에게 상처를 주기도 하고
받기도 한다

힘겹게 보낸 광음(光陰)
되풀이되는 줄 알면서
되풀이한다

세월이 흘러
지키지 못한 약속
유난히 표면화되기를
숨죽이고 기다린다.

Appointment

I open my eyes in the morning
The sun rises

I'm going to live with you
Fear and emptiness precede

With a good smile
With joy
With promises that he cannot keep
You hurt someone
They also receive

The hard-sending light tone
You think it's happening again
Repeat

Over time
An uncomplied promise
Exceptionally surfaced
I wait, holding my breath.

짝사랑

눈을 마주치고
무슨 생각을 하며
바쁜 활동을 하다가
순간적으로
지난 우리의 모습을 들여다본다

남보다 못 생기거나
키가 작거나
가난해서
모난 성격으로
스스로 괴로워하다가
자괴감에 빠진 사랑

삶에 대해 강렬한 참여로
고통과 환희를 수반하고
사람을 짝사랑하고
학문과 진리를 짝사랑하고
우리의 삶을 열렬히 짝사랑하여

마침내, 넓은 세계로 가는
인생 승리자가 되리라.

Unrequited Love

With eyes
With a thought
In a busy activity
Instantaneously
Look into the past

Or worse than anyone else
Short or
In poverty
In a remote character
I'm in trouble for myself
A self-defeating love

With intense participation in life
With pain and joy
You have a crush on people
I love academics and truths
With a passionate crush on our lives

Finally, I'm going to go to a big world
I will be the winner of my life.

미안합니다

고마운 일에는
'고맙습니다'
'감사합니다'를 잘 쓰면서

미안한 일에는
'미안합니다'
'죄송합니다'를 선뜻 쓰지 않는다

그래서
오해를 불러일으키고
못된 사람으로 비치기도 한다

왜일까?
그건 승부 근성이거나
자격지심일 수가 있다

아주 작고 사소한 일에도
'고맙습니다'
'미안합니다' 아니
그보다 더 센 말
'죄송합니다'를 거침없이
쓰는 사회가 그립다.

I'm sorry

For the good of you
'Thank you'
You write 'thank you' well

I'm sorry to hear
'I'm sorry'
I don't use 'I'm sorry very well'

So
Misleadingly
It is also seen as a bad person

Why?
It's either a game-fighting or
Be qualified

In a small, small thing
'Thank you'
'I'm sorry.' No
A stronger word
'I am sorry for you' without hesitation
I miss the society I write.

사랑은 영원히

사랑은 영혼이다

사랑은
이승과 저승을 넘나들며
삶을 영속시킨다

영혼이 떠난 후
초혼(招魂)으로 매번
뜸했던 소식을
삶의 흔적에서 주고받는다

삶의 고통은 사라지지만
진실한 사랑은
마음으로 영원히
그리움으로 남으리.

Love is Forever

Love is a soul

Love
From one world to another
Perpetuate one's life

After the soul has left
With invocation of the spirits of the dead every time
The last news
Give and take in the traces of life

The pain of life is gone
Truthful love
For ever with heart
I'll be missed.

첫눈이

추억과 낭만을 품고
함박눈으로

나뭇가지 위에
지붕 위에
내 어깨 위에

그리움과 사랑을
낳는다.

the First Snow

With memories and romance
With large flakes of snow

On a branch
On the roof
On my shoulder

Longing and love
It gives birth to.

요즈음 미용실

세수하고
머리 감으려다가

어떤 남자들
이발소를 떠올리며
미용실로 발걸음을 옮긴다.

누가 오라나
누가 가라나
누가 미느냐

다 따지고 보면
남자들의 과유불급

임금 같은 남자들을
손님으로 떨어트린 여성시대

값싼 커트를 반기면서도
허전해하는 남자들

등 찜질에
편안한 안마 그리고 면도

아, 옛날이여!

Beauty Salon These Days

Have a wash my face
I was trying to wash my hair

Some men
Recalling the barbershop
I walk to the beauty salon.

Who's coming?
Who's going?
Who's pushing?

After all, I'm gonna tell you
Men's overpaid wages

Men like kings
The age of women who fell as guests

The cheap cut is welcomed
Men who are empty

In the back fomentation
A comfortable massage and shaving

Oh, old days!

문풍지

아득히 먼 옛날

늦가을 우리 가족 연례행사
문종이와 풀
거기에 막걸리까지

날씨 좋은 날
묵은 창호지 뜯어내고
새 창호지에 풀칠하고
문살에 꼭꼭 눌러 붙인다

문손잡이 부분에는
코스모스 꽃잎으로 꽃무늬도 만들고
밖이 보이도록 작은 유리도 붙인다

네 귀가 잘 맞지 않는 문틀 사이로
문풍지(門風紙)도 달아 놓고

올겨울은 얼마나 추우려나?
문풍지 소리가 들리는 듯!

Weather Strip

A long time ago

Our family annual event in late autumn
Paper and grass
And makgeolli

A fine day
Rip open the old window
I'll glue the new windowpane,
Press tightly against the door

The door handle
And make floral patterns with cosmos petals
I also put a small glass on it to look out

Between the door frames where your ears don't fit well
The gate weather strip is attached

How cold is winter this year?
As if to hear the sound of weather strip!

어느 노숙자

보금자리를 잃은 보헤미안
밤과 낮이 무섭다

일출의 설렘도 저녁노을의 아름다움도
집시에게는 두려움의 그림자

생존경쟁에서 뒤처진 그들이
피붙이에게는
가슴 저미는 회한(悔恨)을 남긴다

때로는 노숙자를 측은해하는 마음으로
혐오의 시선을 보내기도 하는 우리는
오히려 미안해야 할지도 모른다

무료급식소에서
행여 아는 이를 만날까
고개를 돌리며
아픔의 한 끼니를 잇는다

지인이 없는 방랑자에게
밤이 두려운 것은 잠자리뿐이 아니다
지나간 난마(亂麻)의 세월이
눈앞에서 춤을 춘다

지하철 바닥에서 막걸리를 벗 삼아
육신을 아무렇게나 눕힌다

절망감으로 생을 마감하자니
부양가족이
서릿발처럼 눈에 꽂힌다

자, 이제 다시 시작해야지
다가올 저녁노을을 위해
천천히 선잠에서 깬다.

A Homeless Man

Bohemian who lost his nest
The night and day are scary

The excitement of sunrise and the beauty of the evening
glow
The shadow of fear for a gypsy

They're behind in the competition for survival
For the blood
The heart beats leave a remorse

Sometimes, with the pity of the homeless people
We are also the ones who give us the look of disgust
It may be something to be sorry about

At a free lunch
I'll see someone I know
Turning his head
Connect one meal of pain

To a wanderer without an acquaintance
Sleep is not the only thing that fears the night
The years of the past chaos
Dance before my eyes

I took off the makgeolli on the subway floor
Lay one's body down in a casual manner

End of one's life with despair.
Dependents
Be stuck in the eye like a frost

Now, we're gonna have to start over
For the coming evening glow
Slowly I wake up from sleep.

달빛으로 피는 박꽃

초판인쇄 2020년 4월 10일   초판발행 2020년 4월 15일

지은이   장현경
펴낸이   장현경   펴낸곳   엘리트출판사
등록일   2013년 2월 22일 제2013-10호

서울특별시 광진구 긴고랑로15길 11 (중곡동)

전화 010-5338-7925

E-mail : wedgus@hanmail.net

정가 12,000원

ISBN 979-11-87573-21-0 03810